For Emelia and Bodhi.
May you always find joy in the now.

If you listen carefully, it can clearly be heard;
the unmistakable call of the White Yellow Bird.

It's not a great sound, it's barely in tune.
A jumble of grumbles, no cheer, only gloom!

He'd get annoyed in the summer, when the leaves blocked his view.
And the sky was always the wrong shade of blue.

He'd moan in the autumn, when the same leaves would fall;

they piled so high,

they made him feel small.

In winter the days were too short and too cold,

and the new life of spring just made him feel old.

In the hope of contentment he collected new things,
like books about flying and the best way to sing.

The problem he found though, from gathering stuff,
was whatever he had never seemed quite enough.

His biggest complaint, was the size of his nest.
When he'd built it he'd thought it was one of the best

But it felt far too small now, even for one,
and it should be on top of the tree, in the sun.

So he rebuilt it up high, where the view was pristine
and nothing could stop him surveying the scene.

But the sun was too much, in the heat of the day.
He started to moan. He needed more shade!

Perhaps the key, to not being sad,
was to compare himself to others and copy what they had.

He saw two happy parrots, what truly dazzling creatures.
Their bright rainbow colours really did set off their features!

His white feathers were dull, and really showed up the dirt,
so he decided a change in colour couldn't hurt.

He made some dye, by squishing up berries,
and covered himself from his beak to his belly.

Bright streaks of red, and purple, and blue.
He left some feathers white, but only a few.

But his 'wing made' dye wasn't so good;
as soon as it rained, it washed off where he stood!

He felt disappointed, that the colour should go,
but at least in the moonlight the dirt didn't show.

He saw birds flying high, and others at speed.

Flying high and fast, he thought, maybe that's the key?

But when he tried flying fast, the wind caught his crest;

he got tired quite quickly, and had to stop for a rest.

And flying up high, just didn't feel right.
Who knew a bird could become scared of heights.

Safely back down, with his feet on a branch,
he started to moan about his options for lunch.
It would have to be seeds again, all the nuts were gone.
Then from deep in the trees, he heard the most beautiful song;

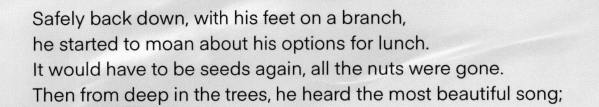

A joyful sound that grew and grew.

The White Yellow Bird wanted to sing like that too!

On closer inspection, the sound that he heard,
was coming from a spindly, scraggly, looking bird;
walking along, without a care in the world,
even though he looked a bit bald.

He didn't have a fancy treetop house;
or multicoloured feathers, most of his were falling out!
He didn't fly high, he didn't fly fast,
instead he moved slowly and stuck to the path.

"Excuse me fine fellow", said the bird white and yellow.
"Could you teach me your tune, it's really quite mellow.

Where did you learn it, did it take long?
It's so nice to hear a cheerful sounding song."

The Scraggly Bird replied with a grin.
"It's easy to learn, just take the day in;
look at the sky, and breathe in the trees,
smell all the flowers, and dance with the bees.

Feel the sun's warmth, or taste the raindrops.
Whatever the weather, the joy never stops"

"Hmm", said the White Yellow Bird, with a sigh.
"It sounds quite straightforward, I'll give it a try."

So he gazed at the sky...

There were too many clouds.

He sneezed at the flowers,

and the bees were too loud!

He looked at the spindly, scraggly, looking bird;
who looked straight back and said only one word.
"Time...
Give it time, my white yellow friend,
each moment's a gift to enjoy till it ends."

He then carried on, at his leisurely pace,
singing his song with a smile on his face.

The White Yellow Bird watched him go on his way,
and then tried once again to take in the day.

The clouds were still there, but only a few.
The breeze ruffled his feathers and felt really quite cool.

He returned, once more, to his treetop nest;
smiled at the view and the sun in the west.

He felt the air in his lungs, and the wind on his wings,
and began to be grateful for the smallest of things.

He let out a call, that sounded much like his own,
but it was far less grumbly, with a little less moan.

"We're all just walking each other home."

Ram Dass, 1931 - 2019

Printed in Great Britain
by Amazon